Channing O'Banning

and the

Turquoise Trail

By Angela Spady
Illustrated by Tammie Lyon

ISBN-13: 978-0615777825
ISBN-10: 0615777821

Library of Congress Control Number: 2013901879
Santa Cruz Press
Leburn, KY

To Steve…
For drawing warm memories
onto my heart.

Table of Contents

Dig In!

"There it is! There it is!" said my best friend, Maddy. She used a paintbrush to sweep away the dirt and get a closer look.

"Are you *sure* we're supposed to use a paintbrush for this?" I asked. "This is weird, Maddy. Very weird."

I wondered if my best friend knew what she was doing. After all, I'M the expert when it comes to using art stuff.

"Oh, but it's NOT WEIRD to keep a pencil stuck in that ponytail of yours?" Maddy

1

asked. I wouldn't talk about weird if I were you, Channing O'Banning!

Maddy did have a point. But I liked to be ready to draw at all times. Having a pencil in my ponytail made perfect sense to me.

"As for my paintbrush, this is how they do it on the educational channel. I'm positive." Maddy continued.

"She's right," Cooper interrupted. "On *Quest for Bones*, they use all kinds of different brushes to sweep away dirt. Once, they uncovered a fossil that was actually a dinosaur egg!"

Cooper always explained every single thing he'd seen on the educational channel. He told us whether we asked about it or not.

"Hmmm....." Coop said, pushing his glasses back up on his nose, "I wonder if cavemen ate dinosaur eggs for breakfast? That would be one BIG omelet!"

Maddy and I stared at Cooper like he was an alien. Sometimes his brain was out on another planet. *Who cared if cavemen ate omelets?*

We got down on our hands and knees and looked closer at the rocks. We'd been digging in the same exact spot for a whole week. On days when it was too cold to go outside, we stayed in at recess and planned our next move.

The whole thing started when Cooper dared me to race him to the end of the playground. Of course, I would have easily beaten him by a mile if I hadn't tripped over a dumb rock! I even tore a hole in my zebra high top sneakers. *It was totally embarrassing.* Not only did I trip on a rock and wreck my favorite shoes— but I let a boy beat me in an easy race. That was just plain wrong.

But the rock that tripped me didn't look like any normal rock. It was gray in some spots, and white in other places. Part of it was sharp and part of it was smooth. So we started digging and digging and digging. There was something really freaky hiding under the Greenville playground. I was sure of it.

We'd even been studying about rocks in Mr. Boring's, uh, I mean Mr. Doring's science class. Boring Doring gave each one a fancy long name that I could barely pronounce. *Why couldn't rocks have easy names?*

"Got any other ideas of what it might be, Maddy?" I asked, anxiously. I couldn't stop thinking about it. I had rocks on the brain.

"Not sure…not sure, Chan," Maddy whispered and continued to brush away dirt. "I wonder if it's some sort of fossil?"

"Really?!" Cooper squealed. "Maybe there are arrowheads under there too! Dig harder, Maddy! Dig harder!"

"Move out of the way, Cooper, and let me get a better look," I insisted. "An artist needs to study these sorts of things, you know."

"Don't be so bossy, Channing O'Banning. If it weren't for ME daring you to a race, or should I say, *beating* you in a race, we wouldn't have made this discovery in the first place."

"Don't remind me." I mumbled.

I looked closer at the dig site and pulled my Gray Elephant pencil from my ponytail. It was times like this that I was glad to have a pencil close by. Plus it looked cool in my ponytail— no matter what Maddy said about it. I drew a picture of our dig site in my sketchbook.

"Mind if we help brush away the dirt, Mad?" I asked quietly. I didn't want to mess up her concentration. This was serious.

"Sure, Chan, but try not to damage anything. This might end up in a museum or something."

"A museum? That would be AWESOME!" Cooper screamed at the top of his lungs.

"Shh...Not so loud!" Maddy whispered. "We don't want the whole school knowing about our discovery yet! Anyway, we have to stop digging and go to social studies class. Bummer."

"Oh, WHY does that goofy bell ring, just when we're getting to the good part?" Coop whined. "I wish we could wait and have social studies class tomorrow."

I didn't mind going to our next class. Social studies was one of my favorite subjects, besides Art, of course. Mr. Reese always made class fun and sometimes even a little crazy. When we studied about ancient Egypt, he came to class dressed up like a mummy (Cooper almost fainted). When we learned about China, Mr. Reese gave everyone a fortune cookie and even showed us how to use chopsticks. No matter how hard I tried, I could NOT get my fingers to hold them the correct way. I almost poked Maddy's eye out just trying to pick up a paper wad!

This week we were supposed to study about Native Americans. That sounded cool too, but Maddy didn't think so.

"Don't be such a grouch. Learning about Native Americans might be fun." Cooper said.

"Not to me. You guys are such nerds. I wonder which Indians he'll talk about today. They all seem the same to me—BOR-ING!"

"Not really, Maddy," Cooper said, as we walked into class. "They're all really different. And they're called Native Americans—NOT Indians. Don't you remember what Mr. Reese said yesterday?"

I could tell that Maddy didn't have a clue. Sometimes she daydreamed in class and didn't pay attention. I often wondered what was going on in that brain of hers. But then again, I daydreamed in class too... sometimes.

"The Native Americans lived here long before we did," I pointed out. "The only reason they were called Indians is because Columbus thought he was in India when he landed here."

Maddy looked a little confused.

"Chan's right," said Cooper. "Columbus was in North America but thought he was way over there!" Coop traced the distance from America to India on a map. "Crazy, huh?"

"Yeah, crazy!" said Maddy. "I guess you could say that Columbus really LOST IT!"

We all laughed at Maddy's joke. Even Mr. Reese giggled a little.

After checking attendance, our teacher had a surprise for everyone. Mr. Reese brought out a small cardboard box from his supply closet and set it on his desk. Maybe we were getting new pencils? Or maybe he'd brought candy for all of us? MAYBE he had gummy turtles for the entire class? Then he'd be my favorite teacher forever!

But Mr. Reese reached inside the box and pulled out three things: a tiny blue rock, a pot with two holes in the top, and a plastic dinosaur. *What was he up to this time?*

Weird. Very weird.

The Mystery Box

"Class, today you're going to learn some interesting facts about Native Americans and the Wild West!" Mr. Reese said.

It did sound sort of fun, especially the Wild West part. I looked closer at the things from the box. I'd never seen a blue rock before. I grabbed a pencil from my backpack and quickly drew the rock in my sketchbook. I hoped Mr. Reese would tell us more about it before the bell rang. I put my pencil in my ponytail, just in case I needed to use it again.

"Remember, kids, there are over two hundred tribes that live in North America. Each has it's own unique way of life." Mr. Reese said, pointing to the large world map.

"Wow," Cooper whispered. "I thought that only the Cherokee and Apache lived in America. I used to watch western movies about them with my grandpa. They were awesome!"

"I guess there's more tribes than you thought," I whispered back. "But if Mr. Reese makes us memorize every single one, I don't know what I'll do. I'm afraid that would be a giant F for flunk-o-rama."

"He won't be my favorite teacher anymore, THAT'S for sure!" said Cooper.

"Told ya. Studying about this stuff is going to be a total brain drain," Maddy whispered, rolling her eyes. "One of these days you people will listen to me!"

Maybe Maddy was right. Maybe we were going to go bonkers with boredom. *But I still wondered about that blue rock.*

Suddenly, I noticed Mr. Reese had stopped talking and was staring straight at us. It was like he had teacher radar and could read our minds.

Yikes.

"Cooper, Maddy, and Channing, would you three like to stand in front of the class and tell us more about Native Americans? You seem to enjoy talking to one another."

I got a lump in my throat and quickly looked down at my neon pink high tops. Maddy buried her head under her social studies book. Cooper froze like a statue.

"As I was saying, there are many tribes in North America. For example, the Zuni live in Arizona and New Mexico," said Mr. Reese. "They create beautiful works of art, including pottery and colorful tribal jewelry.

Channing, would you like to do a poster on the subject?"

HUH?!

"Oh, uh... I guess I could Mr. Reese," I stuttered. "Okay...."

Why didn't Coop and Maddy have to do extra work?

"Another group we'll be studying about is the Apache. They rode horses, hunted buffalo, and lived in amazing tepees," Mr. Reese pointed out.

That's when Cooper freaked out a little. "Oooh! Oooh! I wish I was an Apache!!" Coop squealed at the top of his lungs.

Everyone in the entire class heard him. His face turned as red as the chicken pox bumps he had last year.

"Cooper, would you like to do a report on the Apache?" asked Mr. Reese. "You seem quite excited about the subject."

YES! At least he got busted for talking too!

"I told you Cooper was a big nerd," Maddy whispered. "The next thing we know he'll be building a tepee in his backyard."

But before we knew it, Mr. Reese had given every person in class a ginormous project. This was going to take forever. He must have studied in college how to torture fourth grade kids.

"Are you *sure* the Navajo still exist, Mr. Reese?" Maddy asked, trying to weasel out of her assignment.

"I'm sure, Madison. Once you've completed your report, I bet you'll be an expert."

"Mr. Reese is definitely NOT my favorite teacher anymore," Coop griped. "We'll be working on these projects until we're twenty!"

The clock on the wall said 9:45. We had only a few minutes left.

"Mr. Reese, are you going to tell us more about those things on your desk?" I asked. "The bell's about to ring."

Cooper reached over and poked me with his pencil. "Why are you asking that, Chan? We don't need any more homework! *Geez!!*"

Sometimes Cooper could be so bossy. I tried my best to ignore him.

"Thank you for reminding me, Channing. All of these items are found in the states of New Mexico, Texas, and Nevada." Mr. Reese said, smiling.

He picked up the pretty blue rock and gave it to Cooper to pass around. "Class, this is turquoise, a valuable stone found in the west."

"Hurry Coop! Hand it over! Let me have it!" I insisted, wanting a closer look.

"Now who's acting like a nerd?" Cooper asked, finally giving me the rock. The turquoise felt cold in my hands and had little gray lines running through it, sort of like veins.

Then Mr. Reese picked up the clay pot with two holes in the top. It looked strange, since it had two holes to pour from instead of one. *Weird. Very weird.*

"Hold it gently, everyone. This is a wedding vase made by the Zuni tribe in New Mexico. Before a marriage, the bride drinks out of one side, and the groom drinks out of the other."

The vase was brownish orange with all sorts of special markings around it.

"Don't drop it, Chan," joked Cooper. "You can be a real klutz, you know!"

Why Cooper thought he was funny, I had no idea. I looked closer at the drawings on the sides of the vase. I'm sure they meant something, but I didn't have a clue. If only we could make this kind of stuff in art class.

Mr. Reese held up the last object on his desk.

"This is a model of a tyrannosaurus-rex. These dinosaurs have been found in the West as well."

Maddy didn't even want to look at it. Any kind of dinosaur—even plastic ones— gave her the creeps.

"You can pass that thing on to Cooper. I can see it fine from back here, thank you very much." Maddy said, turning her head quickly.

"It's a TOY! It's made of plastic, you big baby! Why do you have to be such a girly girl?" Cooper joked. "Wouldn't it be awesome to be a paleontologist?"

Maddy look confused.

"You know, one of those people that look for dinosaur bones." Cooper explained.

*Wait a minute…wait a minute…*THAT WAS IT!!!

As soon as the words left Cooper's mouth, a crazy, weird, silly, amazing idea popped into my head: *What if the rock we were digging up at recess was really a fossil of a T-REX?? Or a TRICERATOPS??* It would be the most awesome thing ever! We could be famous!!! We could be rich!!!

I COULD BUY ALL THE COLORED PENCILS THAT I EVER WANTED!

Boring Doring

Science was the last class of the day, which was a total bummer to me. It was my worst subject so I always went home in a bad mood. *Why couldn't every day end with art class?* Now THAT would be perfecto!

But instead, I had to sit and listen to Boring Doring. He could talk for hours and hours about rocks. Blah, blah, blah. Maddy even fell asleep in his class last week. No one noticed until she fell out of her chair with a loud flop. She'd drooled all over the desk and her hair stuck to the side of her head. The whole class, even me, couldn't help but laugh. Maddy never fell asleep in class again.

Maybe today we'd get lucky and learn about the same kind of rocks we were digging up outside. If we were *really* lucky, Boring Doring might even talk about dinosaurs! Hopefully he'd get the hint from Mr. Reese.

"Class, get into your seats, please. We have some very exciting things to do!"

Mr. Boring waved his arms like it was some kind of emergency. "All of you will find out today that school really ROCKS!"

"Science teachers should never try and sound cool. EVER." Maddy whispered.

"You can say that again!" whispered Coop.

Boring Doring's square glasses sat crooked on his nose and his white hair went every which way. He looked like one of those crazy scientists about to bring a monster to life.

"Anyone who likes rocks must have rocks in his head," said Cooper. "Why do we have to study about them? I just want to get them out of our way on the playground."

Coop was right. Rocks were the only things keeping us away from our big discovery. However, I did like the turquoise rock that Mr. Reese showed us in social studies class. Mr. Boring never talked about rocks like that. He only talked about brown, dirty, boring rocks.

"Let's review a little. Who can tell me what a person is called that studies rocks?"

"Crazy!" yelled someone from the back. Jeremy Jackson thought he was the class comedian. He was also the one that bombed every test. Mr. Boring didn't think he was very funny.

"Is it a *geologist*?" I asked, crossing my fingers.

Cooper acted shocked that I knew the answer. Just because I like pencils in my ponytail, doesn't mean that I'm a dingbat.

"Bravo, Channing O'Banning, you are correct!" said Mr. Boring.

Maybe our teacher wasn't as bad as I'd thought.

"Well I know the name for guys who look for dinosaur bones!" Coop said, trying to be a showoff. "They're called PA-LUN-TOL-O-GISTS!"

"That's correct, Cooper." said Mr. Boring. "But it's pronounced PAY-LEE-UN-TOL-O-GIST."

"Why does Cooper think that only GUYS can look for dinosaurs?" I whispered to Maddy. "Who does he think he is, anyway?"

"Oh, Cooper's just trying to be a know-it-all," Maddy said loudly, hoping that Cooper heard her. "He thinks that he's the class brainiac."

Actually, he WAS the class brainiac. Maybe Maddy was a tiny bit jealous.

"Madison Martinez, since you like talking so much, why don't you tell us the three types of rocks in the earth?" Boring Doring asked.

Uh-oh.

I could tell that he didn't think Maddy knew the answer. Maybe he'd gone over that stuff when she'd fallen asleep? This could be bad. This could be *really really* bad.

"Sedimentary, Igneous, and Metamorphic!" Maddy said proudly.

I almost fell out of my chair this time. Our teacher looked as surprised as the rest of us.

"Amazing! That's correct, Madison!"

Cooper and I looked at Maddy like she was from Mars.

"Who are you and what did you do with my friend, Maddy?" joked Cooper.

"Yeah, tell her to come back to planet earth." I added.

"Oh, knock it off, you two," Maddy whispered. "I guess I've dug around in those rocks so much that they're kind of...well...*interesting.*"

"I can't believe it. I CANNOT believe it. Maddy Martinez is turning into a rockologist!" said Cooper.

"A GEOLOGIST!" Maddy corrected him. She bounced a paper wad off his head while no one was looking.

Boring Doring went on and on about the layers of the earth and pointed to a giant poster on the wall.

But. Then. It. Happened. I was starting to get sleepy...*really, really sleepy.*

I could barely keep my eyes open.

"Tomorrow, we're going to study about some very interesting minerals," said our teacher.

My eyelids felt like they weighed ten zillion pounds. I couldn't fight it any longer. I was becoming a sleeping science zombie.

"Everyone should get ready for tomorrow," he said. "You'll be learning all about diamonds, rubies, and turquoise."

TURQUOISE??!!

My eyes flew open quickly. Had Boring Doring talked to Mr. Reese? Did he have a turquoise rock too?

Suddenly the bell rang for class to end. For once I wished that science class could last a bit longer! But I couldn't think about turquoise any longer. I had dinosaur research to do on the computer. That meant that I had to make it home before my big sister, Katie, got there. She was the biggest computer hog around.

If Katie got online first, who knows when I'd solve the dinosaur mystery at the Greenville playground!

Computer Crash

I ran as fast as I could down Darcy Street.

Oh, please, please let me beat Katie home!

By the time I got to the door, I could barely breathe. My legs felt like limp noodles. I needed water...and gummy turtles, of course. But Katie was already sitting at Mom's computer. She even had her feet propped up on the desk.

NOOOOO!

"Do you *have* to be on the computer, Katie?!" I whined.

She gave me her usual eye roll. Sometimes I wished they'd get stuck like that.

"As a matter of fact, I DO need to be on the computer. My friend, Bethany, told me about an awesome song to download. Then I'm going to get online and chat with Mia for a while."

I wanted to scream.

"Katie, all of that stuff can WAIT!" I insisted. "I need to get on the computer NOW! IT'S AN EMERGENCY!"

"Yeah, sure, Chan. Sure it is," Katie said, not believing a single word. "Guess you'll have to stand in line and wait a while, shrimp."

UGH!!!!!!!!!!

But when Katie tried to turn on the computer, it wouldn't even come on. She tried again, and still no luck.

HA! HA!! HA!

"Looks like you don't even know how to USE a computer!" I said. "Poor Katie. Maybe Mom can buy you a plastic one at the toy store,"

"Oh, be quiet, freckle face. I don't think either one of us will be using the computer today. I think it's broken."

"Get out of the way and let me try!" I said. "Let someone try that actually KNOWS what they're doing!"

I pressed the button once, twice, and even three times. Still, it wouldn't turn on. I unplugged the computer and tried plugging it in again.

Still no luck.

"Told ya," Katie said. "Looks like the shrimp can't fix it either."

I had the worst luck ever. The computer crashed and I had zero new facts about dinosaurs. My only hope was to see if Mom could drive me to Nana O'Banning's house. Her computer always worked. But Mom wouldn't be home for over an hour. She had one of those goofy teacher meetings.

My day had taken a nosedive.

I stomped upstairs and flopped down on my bed. At least I had time to get out my sketchbook and draw for a while. I slid out my pencil box from under my bed and found one called Totally Turquoise. SWEET! It was the same name as my new favorite rock.

I imagined I was a famous paleontologist digging in the desert for dinosaur bones. It was so hot that I had to eat ice cream every minute. I drew a picture of me with a popsicle in one hand and a shovel in the other. Then I don't know what came over me. Underneath the rock, I sketched the scariest T-REX ever. It screamed so loud that it blew the pencil right out of my ponytail. I looked into its pink stinky mouth and could count every one of its pointy teeth. My hand froze around my pencil.

"Hey, snap out of it!" said Katie, suddenly. She was always poking her head into my room for no good reason. "You look like you've seen a ghost or something."

At least this time I was glad that my sister had opened her big mouth. I decided to use my eraser and change a few things in my drawing. Instead of making the dinosaur look scary, I colored him purple and drew a propeller hat on his head. I even shared my popsicle with him. I doubt that dinosaurs were purple, or if they ate popsicles. But it was my secret sketchbook and I could do whatever I wanted. Just when I was about to draw another dinosaur, I heard Mom coming up the stairs. *Finally!*

"Hey, Chan. You sure got home from school quickly. Katie said that the computer crashed again. I'm sorry about that."

"Yeah, and if you ask me, Katie messed it up. She never waits for the little hourglass thingy to finish. She just clicks and clicks and clicks!" I said. "Can you take me to Nana's? I really need to use her computer. I'm working on a big project—TOP SECRET!"

"Wow, sounds important," she said. "I need to stop by Nana's anyway. We're having a bake sale at school and I need her advice on a few things,"

"Thanks Mom!" I said, especially about the bake sale part. "Will you make those triple chunk chocolate cookies this time? Those things are DE-LISH! I could eat a dozen in five minutes."

"I'll have to agree with you," Mom said. "But don't let Teeny find out. You know they're his favorite. If that crazy pig gets a hold of them, there won't be a crumb left!"

Surfing the Wave

I could hardly wait to get to Nana's house. Whenever I'm upset, I always grab my sketchbook and go to the Secret Artist Hangout. It's my favorite room in the whole house.

Drawing with Nana always makes me feel better. I once got so upset over bombing a math test, that all I wanted to do was draw black clouds and lightning bolts. But when I got an A+ on a book report, Nana and I celebrated by drawing butterflies and ice cream cones with my Rockin' Red pencil. It was awesome!

Even Teeny gets in on the action every now and then. Nana and I can't quit laughing when he slobbers all over his Piggy Pink pencil. Although I named the pencil after him, all Teeny can do is make a few weird marks on paper.

But the Secret Artist Hangout would have to wait this time. I had some serious internet surfing to do. One way or another, I'd figure out what kind of dinosaur was buried at the school playground. I also had a poster to work on for Mr. Reese's class. I didn't mind doing research on dinosaurs, but didn't Mr. Reese know that I had more important things to do than read about a bunch of Zuni people?

As we pulled into Nana's driveway, Teeny was waiting for me on the front porch. He bounced up and down holding a green pencil between his teeth. Green drool dripped down his chin. I loved that crazy pig.

"Looks like he's been expecting you, Chan," Mom said. "That is one strange pig."

"That is one ADORABLE pig!" I corrected her.

"Hey there, you two!" said Nana, opening the front door. "I hear you're having computer problems at home. Well you've come to the right place! I've already got it turned on so you can surf the wave!"

Sometimes Nana acted a little kooky.

"Remember, Nana? It's called surfing the WEB, not the wave," I giggled. "Thanks for letting me use your computer. I'm on a top secret mission!"

"Top secret, huh? Can you give me a hint?"

"Nope, my lips are sealed!" I said. "But if I solve this mystery, everyone in Greenville will hear about it."

Teeny oinked loudly and ran around in circles.

"Sorry, Teeny, but I can't tell you either," I joked. "You might squeal and tell everyone in town."

"Then get to it!" Nana said, smiling. "Your Mom and I have some planning to do of our own."

I logged on to the computer and typed in my password: COB (for Channing O'Banning). Then I googled: DINOSAURS IN GREENVILLE.

There were zero results.

Maybe it was because no dinosaur had ever been found in Greenville—YET! We'd be the most popular kids in town if we discovered the first one!

Then I typed: WHERE HAVE DINOSAURS BEEN FOUND IN AMERICA?

One website said that they'd been discovered in 35 states! With those kinds of odds, I knew that I was on to something. I tried to think about the mysterious rock that we'd already uncovered. Part of it was gray and bumpy, and part of it was white and smooth.

"Any luck on whatever you're looking for, Chan?" asked Nana. "Remember, I have a ton of books in that shelf over there. I've had some of them since your Dad was a kid."

"I'll look, Nana, but I doubt I'll find anything. Thanks anyway."

I glanced over the shelf and saw books on sewing, gardening, and even one called *Golfing for Grannies*. But just as I was ready to give up and go back to the computer, I noticed a book on the bottom shelf. The dusty old book was called *Prehistoric Creatures That Roamed the Earth*.

Victory!!!

It had tons of dinosaur drawings inside. I studied each one carefully. I never knew so many kinds of dinosaurs roamed the earth. From Ankylosaurus to Triceratops, they were of every shape and size.

But as I flipped through the old pages, one dinosaur stood out more than others: STEGOSAURUS. It had a large hump with sharp things sticking up on it's back. It was smooth in some places and bumpy in others—*just like the fossil at school!* I quickly drew the stegosaurus in my sketchbook with my Chocolaty Chip brown pencil.

"We're finding some yummy recipes in the kitchen," Mom said, popping into the living room. "Want to help us bake, or are you still working on the big mystery?"

"Getting closer, Mom, getting closer!" I said, concentrating on my sketch. "But you guys go ahead and start baking. I'm starving!"

**

"So, if you're not going to tell us about the big secret, let's hear about the big poster that's due soon," said Nana. "What's it about?"

Nana set out a giant plate of chocolate chunk cookies that were still warm.

"Native Americans," I said, with my mouth stuffed full. "Mr. Reese assigned me the Zuni tribe. At least I get to do the art part."

Nana got so excited that she almost jumped out of her sneakers.

"Well, great gorillas!! You have a cousin that lives out west and she collects all sorts of pottery. I'm sure some of the pots are made by the Zuni! How weird is that?!"

"Weird. Very weird," I admitted. "But, Nana, it's not like pottery is real art or anything. And why didn't anyone tell me that I had a cousin out west?"

"Maybe you need to read more about Native American pottery," said Nana. "And as for your cousin, Lyndsey, she's your great aunt Lois's daughter. She moved to New Mexico when you were just a baby,"

I was so confused. I'd never met a Lyndsey OR a Lois for that matter.

"The last time I heard from Lyndsey, she was dating a young man that works at a museum. Maybe I'll send her a z-mail!"

"It's E-mail, Nana, *E-mail*. Not Z-mail," I reminded her for the tenth time. "But I doubt that Lyndsey even knows I exist,"

"Oh, fiddle faddle. Sure she does!" Nana insisted. "She's never met you, but family is family. Once an O'Banning, always an O'Banning! Come to think of it, she sent me a gift last year that maybe you'd like to see?"

Nana quickly went into her bedroom. What on earth could she be up to this time?

Soon she came out holding a small velvet box. Inside was the most beautiful ring that I'd ever seen. There was a square turquoise stone in the middle, and a tiny silver leaf on the side.

"It's beautiful, Nana!" I said. "Did a Native American make it?"

"I believe so. Many of the tribes in New Mexico are wonderful jewelry artists. Would you like to try it on?"

"Really?" I asked. "Are you sure?"

I slowly slipped the ring onto my pointer finger. It was a perfect fit! I rushed to the mirror and held my hand up to my face.

"See, it just fits," said Nana. "Would you like to wear it to school tomorrow?"

Huh? Was she serious?!

"Are you sure, Nana?" I asked. "Are you double TRIPLE sure?"

"I'm double triple QUADRUPLE sure, Chan. Since you're studying about the Wild West, I think it's perfect timing."

I couldn't believe it. Tomorrow I was wearing something to school made by a REAL Native American!

"I'll take good care of your ring, Nana," I promised. "Maddy will go crazy when she sees it!"

Tomorrow was going to be full of surprises. From my turquoise ring to my stegosaurus dinosaur news, it was going to be a day that I'd never forget!!

The Woman
Who Loves Horses

I couldn't wait to get to school. I put on
my favorite striped hoodie for good luck,
and stuck my Blue Raspberry pencil into
my ponytail. It was the perfect pencil
for my big news. As a finishing touch, I
slipped Nana's turquoise ring onto my
finger.

"Are you and your friends going to dig
at recess today, Chan?" asked Mom at

breakfast. "When are you ever going to tell us what you're up to?"

"Sooner than you think!" I said, chomping on an apple. "This is gonna be BIG! I mean really REALLY big!"

Maddy and Cooper just didn't know it yet. I double-checked my sketchbook to make sure that I had my dinosaur drawing.

"What's gonna be big?" asked Katie. She pranced into the kitchen, and grabbed the apple right out of my hand.

"NOTHING," I insisted. Sometimes Katie could be such a blabbermouth. "Is it okay if I go on to school, Mom?"

I needed to hurry before Katie bugged the answer out of me.

"Sure, just don't forget your shovel!" said Mom.

Katie looked more confused than ever.

I grabbed my backpack and raced out the door before the detective could ask any more questions. It was just my luck that Maddy and Cooper were late for school. Of all the days to be tardy, this was not it.

I hung up my jacket in my locker and slid the Stegosaurus drawing into my back pocket. *What if Maddy and Cooper weren't coming to school today?* That would totally stink! When the bell finally rang, I had no choice but to go on to class. My big surprise might have to wait. At least Mr. Reese would make class fun.

"Today is a very special day," said my teacher, smiling. "In a moment you're going to meet a Native American and can ask her any question that you'd like."

Awesome! I wondered if our visitor would be wearing a headband full of feathers or bring a bow and arrow to class? Cooper would go bonkers—that is, IF he'd ever make it to class! After what seemed like forever, my best friends finally stormed through the door.

"It's about time you two got here!" I whispered. "Where were you?"

"Don't blame me," whispered Cooper. "Mom overslept and blamed it on her clock. Then she just HAD to stop and get her drive thru coffee, of all things. Geez."

"Yeah, and they almost forgot to pick me up too!" Maddy added, "But it sounds like we got here just in time. I can't believe we get to meet a real Native American!"

Soon we heard a knock on the door and Mr. Reese welcomed the visitor inside. She looked about the same age as Nana, but with darker skin and long black hair. I couldn't help but notice her turquoise and silver necklace. It had a turquoise flower in the center and silver beads on each side. It was almost as pretty as Nana's ring. *Almost.*

"Class, this is Pelipa Smith," said Mr. Reese. "She's from the Zuni tribe. Pelipa is in town visiting her grandson. Can everyone say hello?"

"Hi Pelipa." Everyone said.

"Keshi," said our visitor. "That means 'hello' in Zuni. Even though my family speaks English, many of us speak Zuni as well."

"Do any of you have any questions for Pelipa?" asked Mr. Reese.

Maddy, Cooper and I looked over at one another and froze. We didn't have a clue what to ask. But then Maddy thought of something at the very same time that I did. She beat me to it by raising her hand.

"My name is Madison. What does Pelipa mean?"

That's exactly what I was going to ask!

"That's a good question," Pelipa said. "In my culture, Pelipa means 'lover of horses.' All of our names have special meanings, and horses were very important to our people.

Pelipa is a normal name for us, just like Maddy is a normal name for your family. "

"There is NOTHING normal about Maddy!" Cooper joked.

"Cooper Newberry," said Mr. Reese, "I think you should remember that we have a visitor and to mind your manners."

Cooper sunk so far down into his seat that I could only see the top of his head.

"Do you live in a tepee, Miss Pelipa?" I asked. "You know, like the Native Americans do on TV?"

"No, I don't live in one of those," she said nicely. "Members of the Apache tribe used to live in tepees long ago, though. I live in a normal house just like most of you. Some of my people still live in adobe houses, however. They're called pueblos. Some have lived there for many many years."

I knew what a pueblo was! Mr. Reese had shown us in our social studies book. I'd even drawn one in my sketchbook.

"Miss Pelipa?" I asked, raising my hand again. "Where did you get your necklace? It's really cool."

"Well, thank you… what's your name?" she asked.

"Channing O'Banning," I said quietly. "I like turquoise rocks a lot."

"So that's why you like my necklace," she said. "I like turquoise too. My grandfather, Lonan, made it for me when I was a little girl. His name means 'Clouds.' I think of him whenever I wear it, because turquoise looks like the sky."

I wanted to ask Pelipa more questions but Mr. Reese made everyone take turns. She told us how corn was very important to her people, and that many of her ancestors traded jewelry with other tribes. If I were a Zuni, I might even trade one of my colored pencils for turquoise. I'd trade Katie in for turquoise if I could.

After Pelipa finished answering questions, the bell rang for recess. It was almost time to tell Cooper and Maddy my big news. I could hardly wait to show them my drawing. Maddy might scream so loud that it cracks the windows in the library. Cooper might even faint. But I knew one thing for sure: we were about to uncover a DINOSAUR!!!

The Worst Day
of My Stinky Life 🖋

We were the first kids on the playground.
Cooper had the shovels and paintbrushes in
his backpack and got ready to start digging. I
was dying to show them my new ring, but my
dinosaur news made me totally forget. I got a
little nervous and my palms got all sweaty.

"Think we'll uncover anything new
today?" asked Cooper. He got on his hands
and knees and began brushing away pebbles.

"We've still got a lot of digging to do," Maddy said. "Chan, did you ask your Dad what he thought might be under here? Since he's a doctor, maybe he can help."

"He takes care of patients, not rocks," Cooper joked. "Right, Chan?"

This was my chance. I took a deep breath and reached into my back pocket.

"Uh, Maddy, Cooper, I think I know what's under there," I said quickly. "I did some research on the computer last night."

Both of them stopped digging and threw down their shovels.

"I think we're digging up a stegosaurus!" I said, and quickly showed them my sketch.

Maddy's eyes got as big as ping pong balls.

"A WHAT-a saurus?" she asked, not having a clue.

"REALLY? A stegosaurus?!" asked Cooper, jerking the sketch from my hand.

"Really, Chan?!" he asked. "Do you REALLY, REALLY think that's what it is?!"

"It's gotta be!" I said bravely, pointing to my sketch. "It has the big humps on its back and it's smooth in other places. It looks just like what we're digging!"

"You're a genius, Channing O'Banning!!" screamed Cooper. "You're a dinosaur drawing GENIUS!"

Maddy jumped up and down and gave me a hug. We all high-fived one another and did a victory dance.

THIS WAS THE BEST DAY EVER!

"Our principal will probably call the newspaper as soon as she hears about it," I said. "They might even print my drawing of the stegosaurus on the front page. This is gonna be B-I-G!"

"They'll probably take our photo!" said Maddy. "I hope they'll wait until tomorrow, since I'm having a bad hair day."

"We'll probably be on TV too!" Cooper said. "Channing O'Banning, you're the BEST!"

"Yeah, you're the BEST!" Maddy agreed. "We gotta finish digging, and FAST!"

We brushed away pebbles as fast as we could and were almost at the bottom. I could already imagine how I'd pose for the photographers. Mom might even buy me a new pair of high top sneakers. Or better yet, a new set of colored pencils. This was the best day of my whole life. *That is, until Katie and her sixth grade friends came by.*

"Whatcha doing, squirt?" Katie asked, trying to show off to her friends.

"None of your business," I said quickly. I wasn't ready to tell her my big news. "Why don't you go hangout somewhere else."

But my pest of a sister totally ignored me.

"Let's see... what do we have here... shovels... paint brushes? What are you babies up to?"

I held my breath, hoping that my friends wouldn't tell her anything. I crossed my fingers for extra luck.

"We might as well tell you!" squealed Maddy. "We've discovered a dinosaur!"

"A STEGOSAURUS to be exact," Cooper interrupted. "It's probably the biggest thing to ever happen at Greenville Elementary!"

"A *what?*" asked Katie. "Yeah, right. You three are such kids."

Katie's friend Andrea moved in to take a closer look.

"There's not a dinosaur down there," Andrea laughed, looking into the hole.

"Sure there is!" said Cooper. "You're just jealous because you didn't discover it!"

Cooper was right. He was the only one brave enough to say it.

"I'm not jealous over a big heap of CONCRETE." said Andrea.

"Huh?" I asked. *"Concrete?"* Perhaps I was hearing things.

"There used to be some monkey bars there. But after Lilly Hoffman fell off and broke her arm, the principal had the monkey bars removed. That heap of concrete is the only thing left."

Katie bent over and laughed her head off. So did her friends.

I wanted to find a closet and hide.

"Concrete?" asked Maddy, angrily. "You thought this was a stego-whatever— and it's *CONCRETE?!!*"

"Yeah!" said Cooper. "What were you thinking, Channing O'Banning?!"

He was more upset than Maddy.

"We did all of this work for nothing! Geez, Chan, you really messed up big time! Remind me never to ask for your help again! Never ever EVER!"

Maddy and Cooper picked up their stuff and went inside. They acted as if I didn't exist. I wanted to go home and hide in my room forever.

Maybe I could join a traveling circus. Maybe Teeny could go too and we'd do crazy pet tricks. He could snort his ABC's after all.

But then something happened that was worse that the dinosaur disaster. When I reached down to pick up my shovel and brush, I noticed that Nana's turquoise ring wasn't on my finger any longer. It was gone! I looked everywhere on the playground. I even traced my steps all the way back to class. It was nowhere to be found.

I was doomed.

What started out as the best day ever ended up being the stinkiest day of my entire life. Not only did Maddy and Cooper think I crazy, but my Nana would never trust me again.

Circus, here I come....

Nana Knows Best

As I walked home from school I noticed that Nana's car was in the driveway. How would I ever tell her that I'd lost the most special ring she owned? I dreaded going inside but maybe Teeny was with her. He always understood. Then again, he was just a pig.

"Hey, Teeny," I said, giving him a hug as he raced to the door. He was covered in flour from head to hoof.

It was easy to tell that Mom and Nana were baking cookies. The house smelled just like a bakery. But for once, I didn't feel like eating. I was too sad over losing Nana's ring. How was I ever going to tell her?

"You're just in time to wash the dishes!" joked Nana. Flour dotted her eyeglasses and I doubt she could see a single thing.

"Hi, Nana," I said sadly, looking down at the ground. I fed Teeny a gummy turtle.

"Only give him *one.* I'm making cupcakes next, and he'll go wild over those too. Heaven knows that crazy pig has a sweet tooth!"

Mom came into the kitchen and put her arm around me. "I have a feeling that *someone* needs a hug today?"

I could tell that Mom already knew about my dumb dinosaur idea. I'm sure Katie the Big Mouth told the entire school.

"I'm sorry, dear," Mom said. "But don't be so hard on yourself. The three of you had fun digging outside. Plus, you got some really good drawings for your sketchbook."

I planned on tearing those sketches into a million pieces. I didn't want any reminder of the most embarrassing moment of my life.

"Mom, how can I ever go to school again?" I asked. "They'll laugh me out of fourth grade! Cooper and Maddy will never speak to me again."

"Oh, fiddle faddle!" said Nana, joining the conversation. "That's plain silly. I don't even know what happened at school, but I know Maddy and Cooper. And I know my Channing O'Banning. You guys are like the three musketeers!"

"The *who*?" I asked, confused.

"Oh, never mind, " she said. "Just know that it will all work out. Have some faith, Chan! Real friends forgive one another, right?"

"I guess so." I said. But I knew what I had to do next....

"Nana, there's something else that happened at school today. It's just…just… HORRIBLE! It's all my fault."

I could feel my heart racing in my chest. I didn't want to look up.

"Chan, it can't be THAT bad. Just take a deep breath and tell us. I love you no matter what."

"Nana's right," Mom said. "Whatever it is, we'll work it out."

If only Mom could be right about this. I took a deep breath and spoke as quickly as I could.

"I don't know what happened, Nana, but I sort of lost your turquoise ring. I had it on my finger one minute, and then the next minute it was gone! I'm so sorry, Nana. I'm very, very sorry. I know it was your favorite." I cried.

Teeny nudged the tissue box over to me.

"Oh… I see," said Nana. "Bu it's okay, Chan. You didn't mean to lose it. At least you told me the truth. See, that wasn't so bad, was it?"

"Do you have any idea where you could have lost it?" Mom asked. "You really need to take special care of things, especially when they're not yours."

"I know, Mom, but I don't have a clue where it could be." I said, sniffling.

"Well, it's over now. Let's just forget about it. We've got some baking to do! How about helping us, Chan?" asked Nana.

I felt so much better after telling Nana the truth about the whole thing.

"Can I help decorate some of the cookies?" I asked. "The snowflakes are my favorite."

"Okay, but only if you've done your homework," Mom said. "I spoke with Mr. Reese about your assignment."

Sometimes it was a real bummer having a Mom that's also a teacher at my school. "I did most of my homework at school. Can't I just decorate one cookie? *Pleeezzee?*" I said, using my puppy dog pout. That usually worked.

"Only one," Mom warned. "And then I believe someone has a poster to work on. Isn't that right?"

Great gorillas! Did Mr. Reese have to tell Mom *everything*? I guess one cookie was better than none. I got the tube of white icing and made all sorts of swirls on the cookie. Then, I grabbed a handful of blue sparkly sugar and sprinkled it on the top. It was almost too pretty to eat.

"You're definitely the artist of the family," said Nana. "That cookie is a work of art! Snowflakes are my favorite too. They remind me of how different and unique we all are."

"You can say that again!" said a pest entering the kitchen. "If there were two of Channing O'Banning, we'd all go crazy!"

Great. My grouchy sister was already home.

Back Your Bags ✏

Something weird was going on. Very weird. Dad was usually home by now and helped me with my homework. I was counting on his help with the Zuni poster.

"Where's Dad?" I asked at dinner.

"Sometimes a really sick patient comes in and it takes more time," Mom explained. "Or perhaps he's straightening up the waiting room. The little ones can sure make a mess of the magazines."

"Can I run next door and check?" I asked. "Maybe he'll let me help clean up?"

"Sure, Chan. And tell him dinner's getting cold."

Dad once paid me three dollars for straightening up the waiting room. I could really use the money this time. I'd decided to try and buy Nana a new turquoise ring. It was the least I could do after losing the other one.

But I had no idea where I could find a turquoise ring in Greenville. I thought about digging for turquoise in my backyard. Maybe I'd get lucky. But one thing was for sure: I would NEVER dig for ANYTHING at school EVER again!

As I opened the door to Dad's office, I could hear him on the phone with someone. "That's wonderful news!" he said. "Congratulations to both of you! We'll be in touch soon!"

What good news? I sure didn't know of any.

"Hey, Chan, what a surprise," Dad smiled. "Are you here for a checkup?"

"No way!" I said, giggling. "I thought I'd come over and see if you needed any help. Oh yeah, and Mom said dinner's getting cold."

"Hmmm. I don't think I need any help at the moment, but thanks for offering," Dad said. "Are you, by any chance, trying to raise money for something?"

Double darn it! Dad knew me too well. I didn't want to tell him the whole story of why I needed money, but I had no choice. As Dad finished cleaning, I told him about the whole nightmare. I started with the dig disaster and ended with telling him that I'd lost Nana's ring.

"That's too bad," said Dad. "But at least you were honest with Nana. That's the most important thing. And the next time I need some help at the office, I'll be sure to let you know."

"Thanks, Dad. I'll have plenty of time to help on Saturdays. I'm sure Cooper and Maddy won't ever ask me to hang out with them again."

"Oh, I wouldn't be so sure," Dad said, trying to make me feel better. "Just give it some time. Winter break starts next week and I have a surprise for everyone!"

"Really?" I asked. "A surprise? Does it have anything to do with that phone call? You sure were smiling."

"As a matter of fact, it does," he said. "But right now, I'm starving. I'll race you!"

Dad took off like a rocket, running out the door towards the house. I quickly rushed past him, jumped over three steps, and made it through the kitchen door just in time. Whew!

"Great gorillas!" Nana said. "You caused me to break the head off of a gingerbread man!"

"That means I can eat it!" joked Dad, reaching to grab the cookie from behind me. "You win, Chan, fair and square. Now go tell everyone to come to the kitchen."

"Is anyone going to tell me what in the world is going on?" Mom asked.

I could hardly wait myself. I needed some good news after having the yuckiest day in the universe.

"The reason I'm getting home late is because I received a call from our cousin Lyndsey."

"Lyndsey?!" asked Nana. "Channing, that's my niece that I was telling you about. Well I'll be a monkey's uncle!"

"You mean a piggy's Nana," Katie joked. "What did Lyndsey have to say, Dad?"

"She's getting married next week. Even though it's short notice, she'd like us to come to the wedding."

"SWEET!" I exclaimed. "But doesn't she live out west? Are we really going?"

"Yeah, can we go?" asked Katie. "We've never been out there before. I'll even be nice to Chan if we can go. Well...uh...*I'll try.*"

"Count me in too," said Nana. "I'd love to see that part of the country again.

"Since it's winter break, and since we haven't seen her in a long time, I say we go for it!" yelled Dad.

YES! YES!" Katie and I said at the same time.

Even Teeny jumped up and down. It almost looked like he was smiling, from one floppy ear to the other.

What a goofy pig.

The Wild Wild West!

I could hardly wait for the plane to land
in New Mexico. I'd never been to the West
before and could only imagine what it was
like. I passed the time by doing a Wild West
drawing in my sketchbook.

I imagined that Teeny and Nana were riding
in a covered wagon like people did long ago.
Mr. Reese said that everyone traveled along the
Santa Fe Trail and that the roads used to be
made of dirt. Talk about a bumpy ride!

I also drew a picture of a Native American and pretended it was me. I wore a shirt made out of buffalo hide and drew a turkey feather in my ponytail. Maybe I was from the Zuni tribe? Or the Apache? Since it was my sketchbook, I could do whatever I wanted.

Teeny slept the whole way on the plane. The only time he woke up was to eat five bags of pretzels that the flight attendant had given him. I couldn't quit thinking about Maddy and Cooper. They didn't even know I was going to New Mexico. I doubt they'd miss me anyway. That dumb stegosaurus ended up being a concrete-a-saurus and a stink-o-saurus.

Maybe I'll hide out in a pueblo.

As I looked out the plane window, I could see red rocks and cactus everywhere, just like in my drawing! But when we finally landed, all I could see was a bunch of buildings. What a bummer. *So much for the Wild West.*

Katie was surprised too.

"Hey, where's all the Cowboys and Indians stuff that you told me about?" Katie asked me. "But I should have known better than to believe you, Channing O'Banning. Or should I say, DINO-GIRL!"

If only I could put a zipper on Katie's mouth. Sometimes she could be downright mean.

"This part of the country has both cities *and* deserts," said Mom. "That's what makes it so unique. Just wait, you'll see."

"There they are! There they are!" said Nana, pointing to the waiting area.

My cousin Lyndsey and her boyfriend Miguel were holding a poster that said WELCOME O'BANNING GANG!

"My, my, Lyndsey's all grown up!" said Nana. "She's so beautiful!"

"And her boyfriend is a HUNKA MUNKA!" blurted Katie.

"Ok, cool it, Katie O'Banning," Mom warned, "Time to calm down."

Katie could be such a weirdo. After exchanging hugs and even introducing them to Teeny, my stomach started grumbling as usual. I was so embarrassed.

"Sounds like someone's hungry?" said Lyndsey. "Do you like tacos? I know a great place close by."

"Can we go, Dad?" I asked. I could almost taste the chips and salsa. "I LOVE tacos!"

"Sure!" said Dad. "I'm starving too. It must run in the family,"

"Channing, maybe while we're waiting on our food, you can show me some of your drawings. Nana says you're a wonderful artist."

Yikes.

I wasn't so sure that I wanted to show Lyndsey and Miguel my sketchbook. *What if they hated my drawings?* But before I knew it, Teeny pranced over to us, holding my sketchbook in his mouth. It fell to the floor and my stegosaurs drawing just happened to fall out.

Uh-oh.

"Wow," said Lyndsey. "That's a wonderful drawing of a dinosaur!"

I could feel my face turn red, purple, and every color in between.

"Oh, uh, thanks, Lyndsey," I said, grabbing my sketch and slapping my sketchbook closed. "I was just doodling one day, that's all."

"I like to doodle and draw as well," said Miguel. "Any reason you chose the stegosaurus?"

But before I could answer, Katie had to open her big mouth.

"I can tell you why!" she said. "You see, it all started back on the playground at school. And Channing thought..."

But just as Katie was about to embarrass me for life, Teeny hopped up in her lap and knocked over her soda. My big sister was soaked from head to toe.

I wanted to kiss that clumsy pig.

"Teeny shouldn't be allowed in restaurants!" Katie said, stomping off to the bathroom. "He doesn't even LIKE tacos!"

"I just like to draw dinosaurs a lot," I told Miguel and Lyndsey. Thanks goodness Katie was in the bathroom. My cousin didn't need to know about my dingbat dinosaur idea.

"Excellent!" said Miguel. "I like them too. Would you like to see some REAL dinosaurs, or at least a cool exhibit of their bones?"

"REALLY?" I asked. "I'd love to!"

"Count us in too!" said the rest of the gang.

Teeny squealed so loud that we had to cover our ears. I guess that meant yes for him too. Lyndsey put her arm around Miguel, causing him to blush as pink as Teeny.

"Did I mention that Miguel just happens to be the curator at the natural history museum? We can go after lunch, if you'd like."

"Yes!" I squealed. *I loved museums!*

"What's a curator?" I asked. "I've never heard of one of those."

"Good question, Chan," Mom said. "A curator is someone who oversees the exhibits at a museum. They get to look at all sorts of interesting things, including different kinds of art."

"Then I'm going to be a curator when I grow up!" I said. "That sounds like the best job ever!"

I could hardly wait to see the dinosaur bones. I wondered which ones were on display. *Anything would be better than staring at a big heap of concrete.*

Dino-Mite

The natural history museum in New Mexico was amazing. Not only did they have stegosaurus, t-rex, triceratops, and pterodactyl bones, but it looked like they were ALIVE. Music even played in the background so that it sounded like they were roaring. I was scared a little, but tried to remind myself that it was just a big heap of bones.

As we walked to the next display, a large sign caused me to stop in my tracks. A big blue arrow pointed to a sign saying TURQUOISE MINE EXHIBIT.

YES! Maybe I could find a piece of turquoise for Nana's ring!

As I walked through the exhibit, I saw every step of how turquoise becomes a beautiful stone. It went from being a plain looking rock, to a shiny blue gem.

"Cousin Lyndsey, do you know where I can buy a turquoise ring? I need to buy a gift for someone special." I whispered.

"Sure, Chan. There are tons of stores in Santa Fe that sell turquoise jewelry. But it can be very expensive."

"Expensive" was not the word that I wanted to hear. I probably couldn't even afford a turquoise ring! I'd done everything to earn extra money– from making Katie's bed to washing dishes every night. If I still didn't have enough money, that meant I'd made Katie's messy bed for nothing.

What a rip-off!

I decided to look at the rings in the museum gift shop. But Lyndsey was right-- they were way too expensive. And it was too late to earn any more money.

"Just be patient, Chan. We have plenty of time," Mom said. " It's time to go check-in to our hotel. It's a real adobe, by the way. Didn't you just study about that in school?"

Mom was right. But I'd never heard of an adobe hotel. *Weird. Very weird.*

Mr. Reese would think it was totally cool. Maybe I'd draw it in my sketchbook and show him when I get back. We had three days left in New Mexico. Surely I could find Nana a ring by then.

As Dad drove north to Santa Fe, we saw the snow covered mountains and the colorful desert. Mom even pointed to a great horned sheep grazing high on a mountain. It's horns curled backwards and it looked like it was wearing a wig.

"Hey, it sort of looks like you, Chan!" joked Katie.

So much for my sister trying to be nice.

"Oh, you're SO funny," I said. "NOT. Maybe we can find your twin out here--a big toothed gopher!"

"Okay, that's enough, girls," Mom said. "Why don't you look out the window at the scenery? Isn't it just beautiful? I can see why the Zuni live here."

Zuni! I'd almost forgot! I still had that poster to do for Mr. Reese's class! It was due as soon as I got back and I didn't have a clue where to start. I needed to find a member of the Zuni tribe—and FAST!

Santa Fe Surprise

Mom was right. Our hotel *was* a real adobe!
The outside was an orangey brown color that
looked like clay. The inside had smooth walls
with woven rugs on the floors. Katie and I
had a room next to Nana's, and it even had
a fireplace called a *kiva*. I flopped down onto
my bed and got out my sketchbook. I drew
a rug with all sorts of lines, zigzags, and
swirls. Luckily I had the perfect pencil, Jelly
Bean Black, in my ponytail. After finishing

my sketch and unpacking my suitcase, I
noticed something strange. Beside our bed
hung a weird leather circle, woven like a
spider web. It had long strands of beads that
hung from the bottom.

"Hey, Katie, what IS this thing?" I asked,
touching the beads.

"Beats me. Maybe it's some sort of animal
trap. Have you seen the size of the lizards
around here? They're ginormous!"

"That's a dumb idea, Katie," I said,
looking at the leather thing closer. "It has
holes in it, genius. I don't think it's a lizard
trap."

As I was still trying to figure it out, Teeny
and Nana came over to check out our room.

"Hey, no fair, you girls have a dream
catcher!" said Nana.

"A *what*?" asked Katie.

"Is that what this thing is?" I asked,
holding it up.

"Many tribes believe that a dream catcher catches all the bad dreams you have at night, and only lets through the good ones. Not a bad idea, if you ask me."

"You said it, Nana," Katie replied. "They must know that I have to sleep with Chan on this vacation. Now, THAT'S a real nightmare!"

"Oh, yeah? Well, they probably know that you snore like a TRAIN and felt sorry for me! There isn't a dream catcher big enough to catch your motor mouth!"

"Okay, okay, time to behave," Nana warned. "It's pretty bad when Teeny behaves better than you two."

I looked at Katie and gave her the meanest look I could. Maybe we could drop her off in the mountains with the big horned sheep.

"Now that we've all rested a bit, how about we do a little exploring?" asked Dad, poking his head into our room.

"I read that they have lots of art galleries here too," Mom said, winking at me. "The Native Americans sell their pottery and jewelry here also."

"Sounds great!" I grabbed my allowance money and stuffed it into my pocket.

"Sounds horrible!" Katie said. " Who wants to look in a bunch of boring old art galleries?"

Why did Katie have to ruin everything? Why did we have to bring her along in the first place? Teeny was way more fun than my grouchy sister.

"Oh, come on, Katie," said Nana. "You might actually have fun and learn a little something."

"Where are we going first?" I asked. "Are you sure that Native Americans really live around here?"

"I'm sure," said Dad. "Lyndsey told me about places to visit. There's even a pueblo where Indians have lived for over one thousand years. It's in a town called Taos. Maybe we'll go there too."

"Awesome! We studied about that in social studies class!"

"Then off we go," Mom said. "After all, you have a poster due when you get home."

UGHHHHHHH! Why did she have to remind me?!!

Shop 'Til You Drop

Mom and Lyndsey were right. There were tons of art galleries in Santa Fe. I kept a pencil in my ponytail and my sketchbook out at all times. One of the stores sold rugs similar to the ones in our hotel. Many were made by the Apache, Cherokee, and even the Navajo!

"Wow, these rugs are awesome, huh Mom?" I asked. "Every single one looks totally different from the others."

"They're a work of art, that's for sure. I really like this one."

Mom held up a black and white rug with a man and woman woven in the center.

"You have good taste," said the storeowner, walking over to me. I noticed the wide turquoise bracelet around his wrist and the beautiful turquoise belt around his waist.

"Welcome to my shop. My name is Ashki and this is a wedding blanket. It's woven by the Navajo to celebrate the joining of two families."

"It's very nice," said Mom. "I'm sure they're very difficult to make."

"It takes months," Ashki said, pointing to the rug. "Here is the bride, the groom, and even their family and animals."

"Are you thinking what I'm thinking?" I asked Mom.

"I sure am," she said. "This would be the perfect wedding gift for Lyndsey and Miguel."

"Even I like it," said Katie.

"Wow, it's a miracle that you two agree on something!" Dad said.

"I'm delighted that you like the blanket. My cousin is the artist that made this one. We're from the Navajo tribe."

"See, Chan, even designing a rug is a type of art. It takes a lot of talent to make something so beautiful." Mom said.

She was right. There were many kinds of art that I hadn't thought of. And I couldn't believe that I'd just met a Navajo! I couldn't wait to tell Maddy and Cooper. But then I remembered that they weren't speaking to me. I tried not to think about it.

In every art gallery we saw something different: rugs, wooden flutes, blankets, and lots of paintings. I wished my art teacher at Greenville could have seen it.

"Hey, can we go in this store, Nana?" I asked. "It looks like it's got some cool stuff. I crossed my fingers that there was jewelry for sale.

When we walked inside, there were tons of clay pots of every shape and size. Some had birds painted on them and some had lines going in every direction. I couldn't imagine how they painted such tiny designs on each pot.

"Teeny, don't you dare touch anything in here!" warned Nana. "See the sign? It says, YOU BREAK IT, YOU BUY IT. I don't think you have any cash, so *behave.*"

Teeny must have known that Nana meant business. He walked quickly over to the corner and sat on his hind legs without the slightest snort.

While I looked around, I couldn't help but think about Mr. Reese and the vase he'd shown us. At that exact moment, I looked up on the top shelf and saw something familiar. There was a whole row of wedding vases!

They looked just like Mr. Reese's, only bigger. The one I liked the best had black wavy lines painted on it. The tag said "MADE BY LUSITA. ZUNI TRIBE."

"Yes!" I squealed. "Nana, this one is made by a Zuni!"

I quickly drew it in my sketchbook.

A pretty lady with a long black braid came over to check out what I was doing. She looked about Mom's age and wore a colorful dress with a fancy leather belt.

"That's a wonderful sketch," she said, nicely. "My name is Elu. My sister, Lusita, made the vase you're drawing."

"I know what kind it is! It's a wedding vase, isn't it? The groom drinks out of one side and the bride drinks out of the other!"

"Very good. You are correct," she said.

"Wow, Chan. I had no idea you knew that," said Nana. "Elu, please tell your sister that she makes beautiful pots."

"Yeah, tell her from me too!"

"Would you like to tell her yourself?" Elu said. "She's in the back making more pottery. Would you like to see?"

"Sure! Can we, Nana? Please?????"

"I don't know why not! I'd like to see that myself. Teeny, stay put. Don't move one hoof."

We walked towards the back of the store, into a small workshop. Lusita was rolling clay into long skinny pieces. It didn't look anything like a pot.

Weird. Very weird.

"This is how Lusita begins. We call this coil pottery. She puts one coil on top of the other and smoothens them together."

"Hello," said Elu's sister. "Who do we have here?"

My throat got dry and my tongue froze. I was getting ready to speak to a real Zuni artist.

"Uh...my name is...is..." I suddenly couldn't remember my own name!

"I'm Channing...Channing O'Bannning. But you can all me Chan."

"That's a pretty name," she said. "Would you like to help me make a pot?"

Did she just say what I thought she said? It sounded like she asked me to help.

"I need someone to roll out the coils. It's sort of like rolling cookie dough into a log. Would you like to try, Chan?" asked Lusita.

"Sure!" I said, hopping onto a stool. After watching Lusita first, I wet my hands with water and rolled out the clay. It was harder than it looked! Lusita placed each coil on top of the other and connected them at the ends. Then she took a little wooden tool and smoothed them together. She made it look so easy.

"After this, we'll put it into a kiln, which is very, very hot. Then I will paint it and heat it again."

"Wow, making a pot is a lot harder than it looks!" I said. "And I thought drawing with my colored pencils was tough."

"You're right," said Lusita. "And every pot is different. Every design is just as special as the other."

"Wow, I never thought of it that way." I said.

"It's true, you know," said Nana. "I think I'll buy this one for Lyndsey and Miguel. They'll love knowing that you helped make their wedding vase. Now, if we can just find Teeny. Let's just hope he isn't stuck in a pot, snout first!"

The Turquoise Trail

When we met back up with the rest of the gang, I barely recognized Katie. Her blonde hair was tucked under a cowboy hat and on her feet were a pair of sparkly red cowgirl boots. They weren't as cool as my purple high top sneakers, but they were pretty awesome.

"So much for you thinking that New Mexico was boring!" I reminded her. " Did you get lost in a wild west clothing store? You fit right in here."

"Yeah, this place is pretty cool," said Katie. "And guess what? The guy that sold us the boots told us about a place where you can dig for turquoise. He even gave us a map."

"Let's go, let's go! Where is it?! Where is it?!" I squealed.

My luck might be turning around.

"Calm down," Katie said. "It could be far away, for all I know. But it's on a road called The Turquoise Trail. I guess that's a good sign?"

"Sounds like a place worth checking out," Mom said. "Let's all pile into the van and try to find it. You too, Teeny!"

Dad took the map and Mom gave him directions on where to turn. After driving several miles, we finally noticed a sign that said THE TURQUOISE TRAIL.

"There it is! There it is! It says turn right!" I pointed out. "Go there Dad!"

"Okay, I see it. It's on up ahead," Dad said. "But remember, we have to get back to Santa Fe soon. Lyndsey's wedding is tomorrow."

After driving a little further on the Turquoise Trail, we noticed a storefront with a flashing blue sign: MINE TOURS SOLD HERE. My heart started racing.

"Dad, we have to stop! Please!" I begged. "It's a museum too!"

I checked to make sure that I still had my allowance money. This was my best chance yet to find a piece of turquoise for Nana's ring.

Before we could explore the mine, we had to watch a video called The History of Turquoise. *I didn't have time to watch a movie! I had a rock to find!*

But it was way more interesting than I'd thought it would be. I saw pictures of fancy turquoise jewelry worn by real Zuni princesses and warriors.

"I wish I was a Zuni princess." I whispered to Katie.

"Yeah, me too," she agreed. "I've never seen jewelry like this before. Not even at the mall."

"Duh," I shot back. "This jewelry is special. Right, Dad?" I asked.

"Right, Chan. Many tribes pass their beautiful jewelry down to other family members, too."

That reminded me all over again that I'd lost Nana's special ring. I felt horrible all over again.

"Dad, can we go look for turquoise now? Please??"

The mine was huge and hard to climb. I walked around and around turning over one rock after another. None of the rocks looked like turquoise to me. The guide showed us what to look for, but I couldn't find a thing. The rocks looked as dull as the ones at school. I looked at rock after rock, trying to find a blue one. Even Teeny tried to help, and used his snout to sort through the pebbles.

"Thanks, Teeny, but I'm afraid it's no use," I said, scratching his ear. "This was a crazy idea."

"You can say that again. It's almost as crazy as you trying to dig up that concrete monster at school!" Katie shouted.

"Oh, be quiet, Katie! You're such a—"

But suddenly, out of the corner of my eye, I saw a hint of blue.

Could it be? Could it really truly be?

I pushed Katie out of the way, picked up the rock, and took it to the tour guide.

"Well, I do believe you've found a piece of turquoise!" she said. "See the sky blue line there? Once it's cut and polished, you'll have a precious little stone."

"Can you cut and polish it here?" I begged. I crossed my fingers and toes. I was running out of time.

"As a matter of fact, we have a jewelry shop that can help you. But it won't be finished until tomorrow."

"Can you make a ring out of it?" I whispered into her ear. I made sure that Nana was nowhere around. "It's a surprise for someone special. Is this enough money?"

"Since you found your own turquoise stone, you'll have just enough. And your secret's safe with me," said the tour guide. "I'll even pinky promised to make it official."

"What are you two locking pinkies about?" asked Nana. She had an armful of rocks, and looked worn to a frazzle. "I've looked at every one of these crazy rocks and can't find a single thing!"

Nana's glasses were half off and her hair was a mess. "This turquoise hunting is for the birds! Are you SURE this is a turquoise mine?" she asked. "I'm pooped!"

"I'm sure, Nana," I said giggling at my grandmother. "I'm absolutely sure."

Here Comes The Bride

Our trip to the southwest was one of the best vacations ever. From looking at dinosaurs to digging in a turquoise mine, New Mexico was my new favorite place. And to top it all off, we were going to Lyndsey and Miguel's wedding. A giant slice of wedding cake was in my future.

Nana made sure that the wedding vase was wrapped tightly, so it wouldn't break.

"Teeny, if you put one pink hoof on that box, you're in big trouble!" she warned.

"There will be NO gummy turtles for you ever again."

"You'll be good, won't you, Teeny?" I said, patting him on the head.

I'd even given him a bath and he was clean as a whistle. He smelled like bubblegum.

"Mom, do you need me to help wrap the Navajo Wedding Blanket?"

"Thanks, Chan. But the nice man at the shop wrapped it. He even included a paper that shows what each design means. Lyndsey and Miguel should enjoy reading it."

**

The whole church smelled like a flower shop.

Miguel's family sat on one side and Lyndsey's family sat on the other. That didn't make sense at all.

"Why can't we sit wherever we want?" I asked Mom. "This seems weird. Very weird."

"Yeah, how can Lyndsey's and Miguel's family get to know one another if they have to sit in different places?" Katie asked.

"This is just part of a wedding tradition," Nana explained. "Lyndsey and Miguel's family will have lots of time to meet one another."

"I won't have wedding rules when I get married!" said Katie.

"Don't worry, Katie," I giggled. "No one will marry you anyway!"

"Now who's trying to be funny?!" she said. "Let's have a truce. No more mean comebacks. Deal?"

"Okay, okay...*I guess*," I promised my sister.

The piano music began playing and a few of Lyndsey's friends walked to the front of the church. Each girl held a pretty red flower with a yellow ribbon.

Miguel looked a little nervous, like he might faint. But then Lyndsey walked in. She looked amazing. Her dress was covered with white lace and pearls, and she even had white flowers in her hair like a princess.

After what seemed like forever, the minister finally said, "I now pronounce you husband and wife."

FINALLY!

Miguel gave Lyndsey a mushy kiss, and Nana and Mom cried like big babies. *Geez.* All I could think of was the wedding cake.

"I'd like a piece with a big rose on top!" I told the lady serving the cake. "And vanilla ice cream, please."

The lady even cut two pieces for Teeny. He looked so cute in his little black bow tie.

"Welcome to our family, Miguel!" said Dad. "It was a beautiful wedding!"

"Gracias, thank you, Dr. O'Banning. You must visit us again. Channing, maybe there will be a new dinosaur exhibit at the museum next time. There might even be a Mesosaurus. Those dinosaurs—"

"Used to swim in water!" I said. "I know about them too!"

"Very good, Channing O'Banning. You're a regular dinosaur expert!"

Miguel motioned for me to come closer, like he had a secret for me. "I know the lady at the turquoise mine and she said this box was for you."

I quickly peeked inside. They'd finished Nana's turquoise ring! The stone was polished and shiny, and the ring even had a silver leaf on the side. It looked almost like the one that I'd lost.

"Thanks, Miguel! Gracias, gracias!" I said, giving him a hug. Lyndsey wasn't the only one getting a beautiful ring today.

I could hardly wait to find Nana.

Lost and Found ✏️

"Oh, Nana, I have a little something for you!"
I said. "Now, close your eyes and hold out
your hands!"

I could hardly wait to show her. *What if
she didn't like it?*

"For me?" squealed Nana. "Chan, what on
earth are you up to?"

I placed the box into her tiny hands and
she untied the bow slowly.

"Oh my! It's beautiful! It's absolutely beautiful!" Nana gasped and slid it onto her finger. It just fit.

"That's to replace the one that one that I lost at school." I reminded her.

"That is so nice of you, Channing. But you didn't have to do that. I forgave you for losing it. And guess what, I have a surprise for you too!"

Nana reached into a small bag and handed me a new pencil called Adobe Orange. But something special was also tied around the pencil: it was a silver and turquoise ring! It looked just like Nana's only smaller.

"Wow!" I said. "It's awesome! Now we match! And I don't have this color of pencil either. I'll use it on my poster for Mr. Reese's class. I'll take extra good care of both of these things, Nana."

"Good minds think alike," said my grandmother. "I'm glad that my little artist likes both of them. Now let's get ready to make one last stop to see the Taos Pueblo. You'll want to draw it in your sketchbook for sure!"

I stuck my new pencil into the top of my ponytail, and slid my new ring onto my finger. After riding in the backseat with Teeny for a while, we finally made it to Taos. Dad pulled the van in front of the largest pueblo that I'd seen yet.

"We don't have much time, but we can't go back to Greenville until we've seen this very special place." Said Dad.

"I studied about this at school, but I didn't think I'd ever see it for real," I said. "There's a picture of this in my social studies book."

"Well then, would you like to tell us all about it?" asked Mom. "I'm sure Mr. Reese would be proud of you."

I went on to explain that Indians had lived here for over one thousand years. There was no electricity in the pueblo, and they drank water from the little creek out front. The water came all the way from a special lake that was very important to them.

If only Maddy and Cooper could have seen the Taos Pueblo. But they'd never forgive me for the dinosaur disaster, so they certainly wouldn't believe that I'd seen this famous pueblo. Just thinking about them made me sad all over again. I wished I could stay in New Mexico.

There had to be a pueblo around for embarrassed artists, somewhere.

**

As soon as we got home, I raced to my room and got out my sketchbook and pencils. My poster assignment was going to be a breeze after all that I'd seen in New Mexico.

But I super dreaded going to school the next day. I didn't even touch my pancake topped with gummy turtles.

"Chan, I know you don't want to see Maddy and Cooper. But I'll bet they've already forgotten all about the...well, you know...the dinosaur mix-up."

"I hope you're right, Mom. My stomach is kind of queasy. Maybe I'll wait and go to school tomorrow."

"You'll feel better once you get to school," Mom said. "Now scoot, or you're going to be late."

As soon as I got there, the first two people I saw were Maddy and Cooper at the lockers.

Yikes.

"Uh, hi, Maddy," I said quietly, looking down at my sneakers.

"Hey, Chan! Where did you go on winter break? I tried calling you a dozen times." Maddy said.

"Huh? *You did*?" I asked.

"So did I," said Cooper. "Did you vanish, or what?"

"You two really wanted to talk to me?" I asked. "I didn't think you'd ever speak to me again, after the....well...you know."

"Oh...THAT," said Cooper. "Maddy and I talked about it and we're over it."

"You are?" I asked happily. "You mean you forgive me?!"

"Sure we do, silly. After all, it *was* kind of fun digging around in those rocks and stuff. Even if it was just a piece of concrete." Maddy said.

"And we have a surprise for you!" said Cooper.

Whew! It was such a relief to have my best friends back. Mom and Nana were right all along. Suddenly, Cooper reached into his pocket and held out his hand. I could hardly believe my eyes.

It was Nana's ring.

"You found it! You found it!" I screamed. "Where was it?"

"It must have slipped off your finger when you were digging. I found it right after school."

Now Nana would have two rings!

"Coop, you're the best!" I said, giving him a high five. Not only did my friends forgive me, but they even found Nana's treasured ring in that crazy concrete mess.

"Chan, are you ever going to tell us where you've been?" Maddy asked, as we walked to class.

"I went to my cousin's wedding in New Mexico," I said. "Mr. Reese was right— the Wild West is a cool place. You won't BELIEVE the tons of dinosaurs they have out there!"

Maddy and Cooper looked at each other and smiled. I knew exactly what they were thinking....

But this time I took a picture!

The End

Want to read more about Channing O'Banning?
Check out www.channingobanning.com and find out where the famous fourth grade artist is going next!